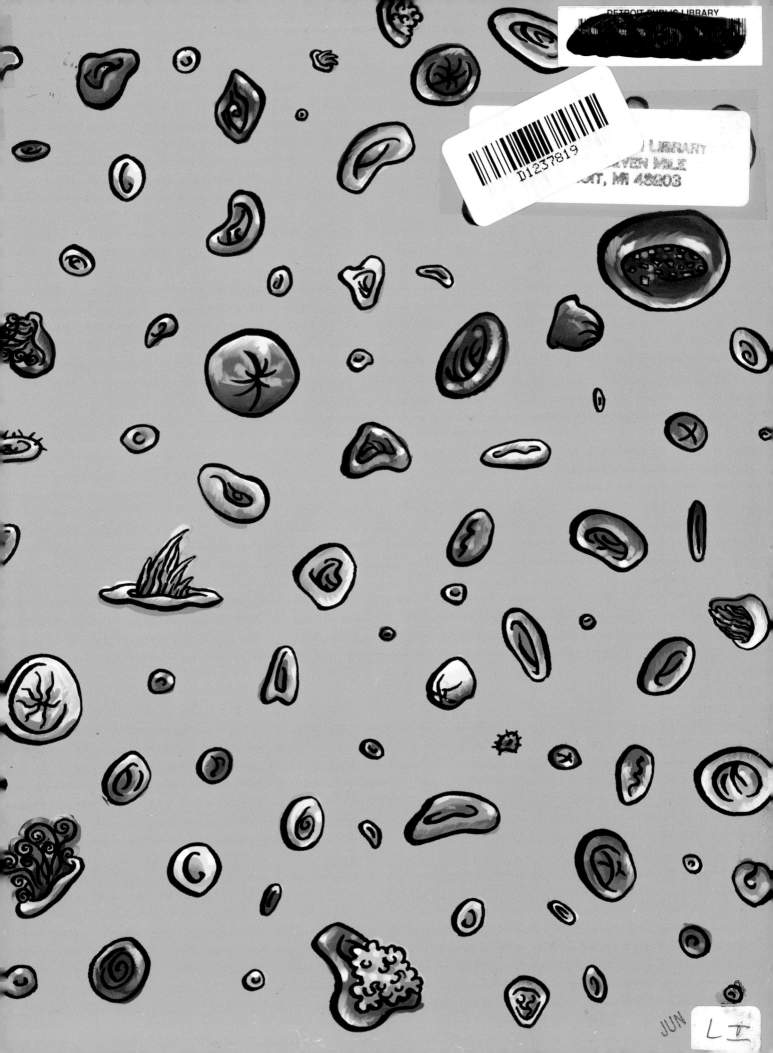

To every child who has a belly button-and a keen imagination.–BN & SN

To my beautiful girls Jane and Sadie and their perfect "buggybuttons".–BH

Published 2008 by August House LittleFolk
3500 Piedmont Road NE, Suite 310, Atlanta, Georgia 30305,
404-442-4420
http://www.augusthouse.com

Manufactured in Korea

10 9 8 7 6 5 4 3 2 1

Library of Congress Cataloging-in-Publication Data

Norfolk, Bobby, 1951-
Billy Brown and the Belly Button Beastie : inspired by a Japanese
folktale / as told by Bobby and Sherry Norfolk ; illustrated by Baird Hoffmire.
p. cm.
Summary: Billy Brown, having failed to heed his mother's warning to
stay covered while he sleeps, awakens one morning to find his
perfectly round brown belly button gone, and then tries to trick the
Belly Button Beastie into giving it back.
ISBN 978-0-87483-831-2 (hardcover : alk. paper) [1. Belly
button--Fiction. 2. Monsters--Fiction. 3. Bedtime-- Fiction.] I.
Norfolk, Sherry, 1952- II. Hoffmire, Baird, 1969- ill.
III. Title.

PZ7.N7766Bil 2008
[E]--dc22
2007034115

Lesson plans available at augusthouse.com.

August House, Inc.
A T L A N T A

Billy Brown and the Belly Button Beastie

inspired by a Japanese folktale

as told by Bobby & Sherry Norfolk

illustrated by Baird Hoffmire

AUGUST HOUSE
Little folk

Atlanta

Billy Brown had chocolate brown skin. He had curly black hair. He had big brown eyes and a round brown belly—and right in the middle of his round brown belly, he had a round brown belly button.

Every night, Billy Brown's mama tucked him in bed. Every night she said, "Don't you go kicking off those covers, or you'll catch cold!"

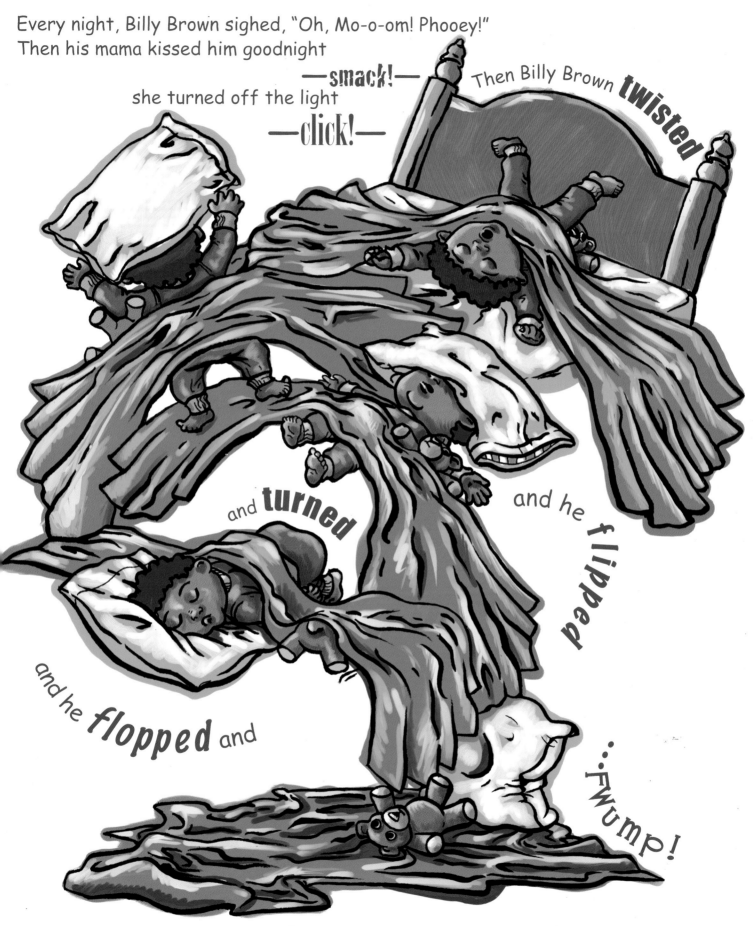

Every night, Billy Brown sighed, "Oh, Mo-o-om! Phooey!"
Then his mama kissed him goodnight

—smack!—

she turned off the light

—click!—

Then Billy Brown **twisted**

and **turned**

and he **flipped**

and he **flopped** and

...Fwump!

—he kicked off the covers.

One night Billy Brown's mama said,
"Don't you go kicking those covers off tonight.
If you do, the Belly Button Beastie is going to come and take
your belly button right ... out ... of your ... BELLY."
Billy Brown sighed, "Oh, Mo-o-om! Phooey! You can't scare me!
There's no such thing as a Belly Button Beastie!"

His mama said, "I wouldn't go trying to find out if I were you, Billy Brown." Then she kissed him goodnight—**smack!**— she turned off the light—**click!**—

Billy Brown called after her, "I'm not scared of any Belly Button Beastie, because there is no such thing ... I hope!"

Billy Brown kept the covers up under his chin that night.
He held on tight and did not move until he started to fall asleep.
Then he began to **twist**. And **turn**.
And *flip*. And *flop* and

—FWump!

He kicked off the covers ...

... and went to sleep.

ThWump! He did not see the Belly Button Beastie's face, with its two squinty eyes and its drippy nose and its slobbery mouth and its floppy ears. He did not see the Belly Button Beastie's bag, or hear him sing in a creaky, screechy voice,

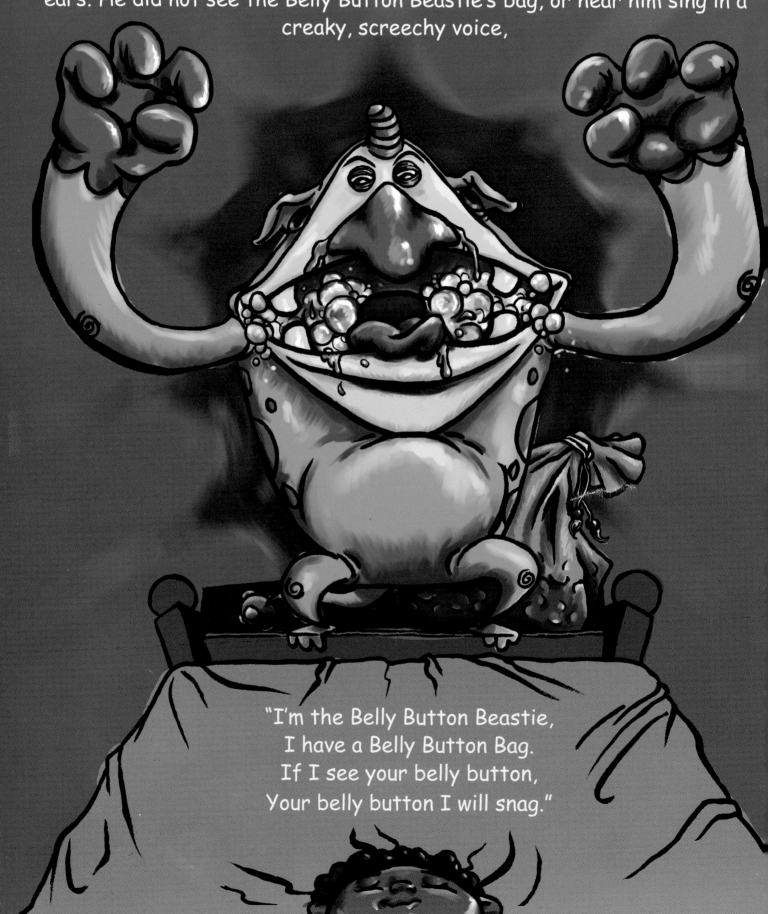

"I'm the Belly Button Beastie,
I have a Belly Button Bag.
If I see your belly button,
Your belly button I will snag."

He did not see the Belly Button Beastie's finger come closer and closer until—**scronk!**—it took Billy Brown's belly button right out of his belly!

"Wow!" gloated the Belly Button Beastie. "This really IS a perfectly round brown belly button! It's the very best belly button in the whole belly button bag!"

The Belly Button Beastie plopped Billy Brown's belly button into the belly button bag and—Thwump!—he disappeared.

In the morning when Billy Brown woke up, he felt
perfectly normal.
He went to the kitchen, poured a glass of milk,
and drank it.

Billy Brown heard a funny sound.
Bloop, bloop, bloop!
He felt something cold and wet trickling down his belly.
He looked down.
The milk was coming out of a hole in the middle of his belly!

"Oh no! There really
IS a Belly Button Beastie! It
got my belly button! What am I
gonna do?" Billy Brown ran around
the kitchen clutching his belly to keep
the milk from running out of the hole.

Then he stopped.
What was his mother going to say?
Billy Brown stood still for a
moment and thought.

"I'll take a bath. If I clean up all the milk, Mama will never know!"

So Billy Brown started a big bubble bath and climbed in.
"Ah-h-h-h!"

He closed his eyes and began to relax. Bloop, bloop, bloop! The bubbles were pouring into the hole in his belly! **Bloop–bloop–bloop–bloop–bloop!** His belly was filling with soapy water! "I can't go to school like this! I've got to get rid of these bubbles!"

Billy Brown began to squeeze his belly
—*Bloop-bloop-bloop-bloop-bloop!*—
until all the bubbles were out and floating
around the bathroom.

It took every single towel in the
house to clean up the mess, but Billy
Brown finally got dressed
and out the door.

When Billy Brown got to school, his friends stared at him.
"Billy Brown, you look SICK!"
"Look at THIS!" said Billy Brown, and he lifted his shirt.
"Billy Brown, your belly button is missing! What're you gonna DO?"

"I don't know," moaned Billy Brown. "When I drink anything, it comes right out the hole. If I sit in water, it pours in. I think I'm gonna die!"

"Don't give up," his friend said. "Try this." He reached into his
pocket and pulled out a small piece of chocolate.
Billy Brown looked at it sadly.

"It's no use," he said. "Nothing's gonna work."
He stood staring at the chocolate—then his face lit up.

"Wait! If I can't stop up the hole in my belly with this, I can use it to trick the Belly Button Beastie into giving me back my own round brown belly button!"

Billy Brown unwrapped the chocolate.
It matched the color of his chocolate brown skin.

"Now let's see how it looks."
He put the chocolate into the hole in his belly.
It looked exactly like his own round brown belly button

—but it smelled a whole lot better.

That night Billy Brown got into bed and pulled the covers up to his chin. He began to **twist** and **turn** and *flip* and *flop*. Then he called out, "I sure hope the Belly Button Beastie doesn't find out I have a NEW, even BETTER, round brown belly button!"

Then—FWump!—he kicked off the covers and pretended to go to sleep.

The Belly Button Beastie's finger came closer and closer ... but just before it reached Billy Brown's new round brown belly button, Billy Brown sat up and shouted, "**Boo**!"

The Belly Button Beastie screamed. It began to **shiver** and **shake**. "You scared me! Why'd you go and do a thing like that?"

"I want my own round brown belly button back, that's why!"
snapped Billy Brown.

"No-o-o-o! I never ever, ever give back belly buttons. But—"
SNIFF! Sniff-sniff!
" —that sure does smell good! Gimme, gimme, gimme!"

"No!" yelled Billy Brown. "I'll trade you. You can have this belly button if you'll give my old one back."

The Belly Button Beastie thought. He sniffed some more and thought some more.

"I'll make you a deal. If you can find your belly button in my belly button bag, we'll trade.
But if you can't, I get them both!"

"Deal!" shouted Billy Brown.

The Belly Button Beastie opened up the belly button bag, and Billy Brown looked in. There were THOUSANDS of belly buttons in the belly button bag! There were hairy ones and slimy ones, stinky ones and fuzzy ones. There were different shapes and sizes and colors. Billy Brown was just about to give up when —"GOT IT!"—he pulled a perfectly round brown belly button out of the belly button bag.

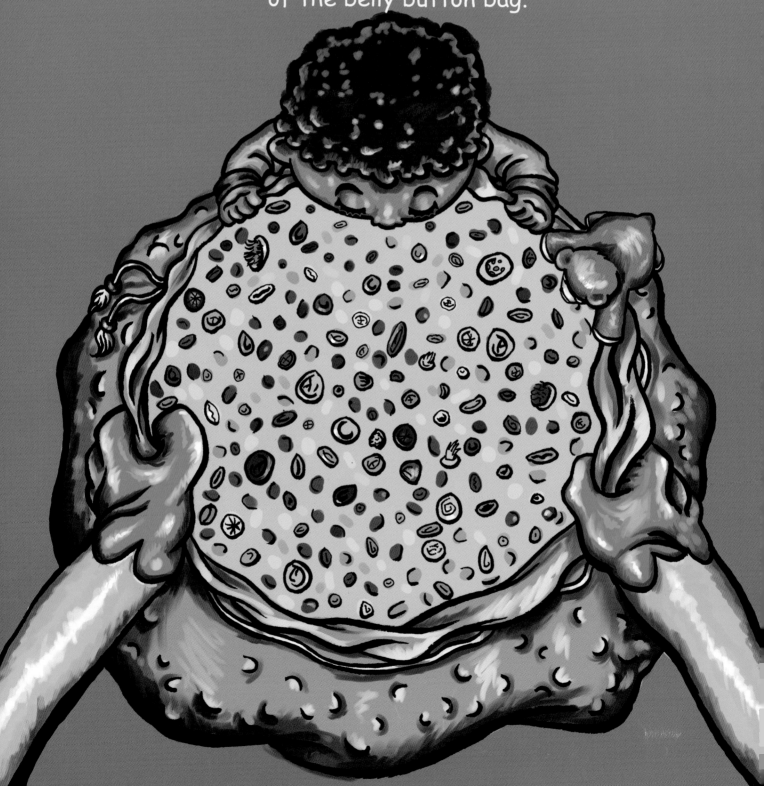

"Now I have to make sure it still works," said Billy Brown.
He took out the chocolate and put his own
round brown belly button in its place.
Then he drank a whole glass of water.
Nothing happened!

"It works!" shouted Billy Brown. "Here you go!"
The Belly Button Beastie took the piece of chocolate.
SNIFF! Sniff-sniff! Gobble-gobble-gobble-gobble-gobble!

And he disappeared. ThWump!

Ever since that night, the Belly Button Beastie
has never stolen another belly button.
But if you have a piece of chocolate lying around
—you better watch out!

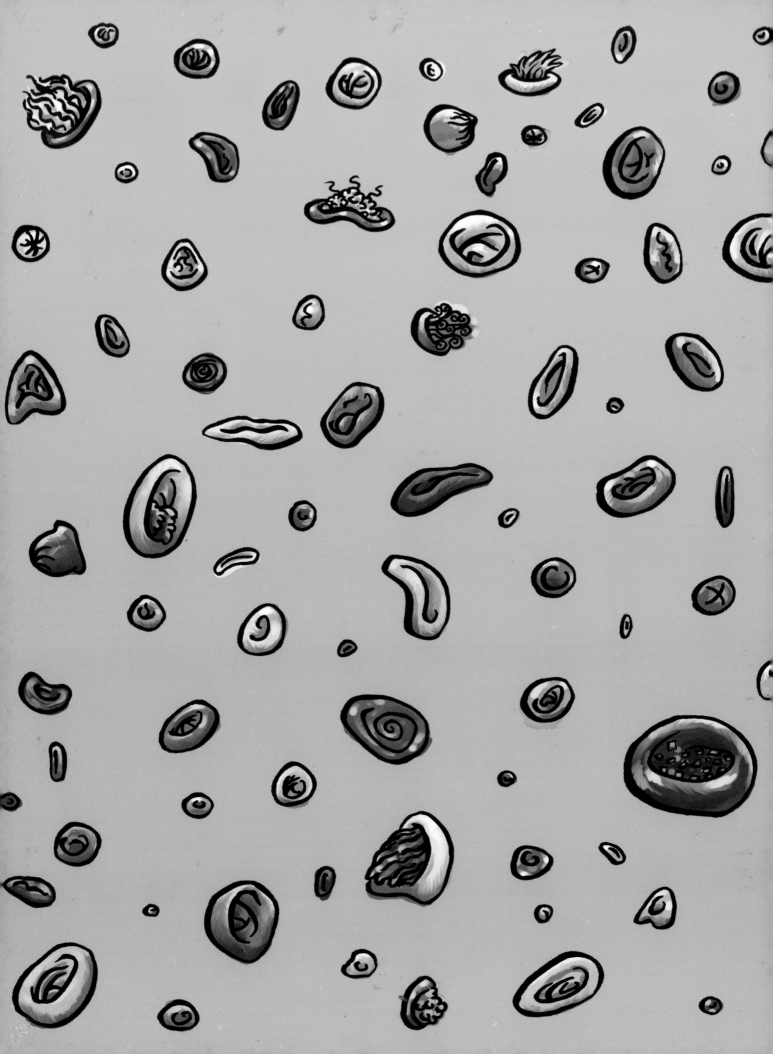